Wagon trains at Independence Rock
Painting by W.H. Jackson, 1929
UTAH STATE HISTORICAL SOCIETY

1

"The Sentinel" (detail) by Frederic Remington, 1907

FREDERIC REMINGTON ART MUSEUM, OGDENSBURG, NY

THE
OREGON TRAIL

by

LEONARD EVERETT FISHER

Holiday House/New York

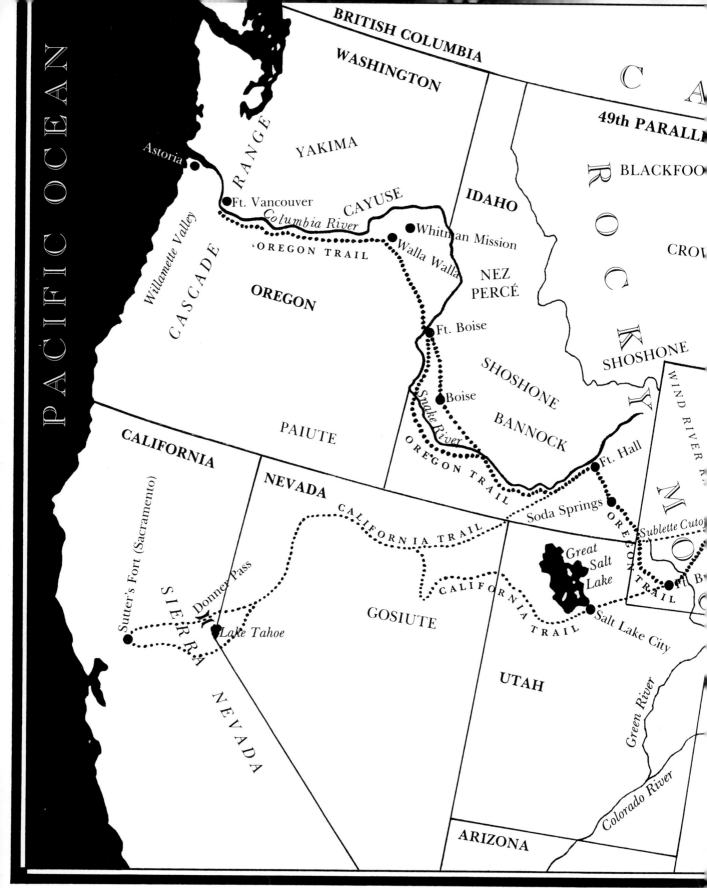

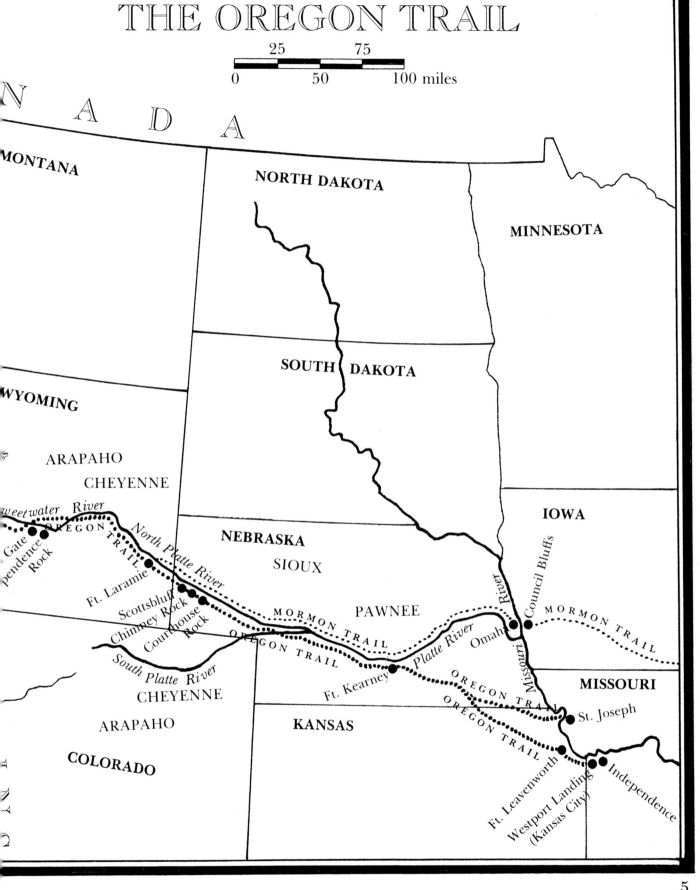

THE OREGON TRAIL

25   75

0   50   100 miles

NADA

MONTANA

NORTH DAKOTA

MINNESOTA

WYOMING

ARAPAHO

CHEYENNE

Sweetwater River

OREGON

Gate

pendence
Rock

OREGON TRAIL

North Platte River

Ft. Laramie

Scottsbluff
Chimney Rock

Courthouse
Rock

South Platte River

CHEYENNE

ARAPAHO

COLORADO

NEBRASKA

SIOUX

PAWNEE

MORMON TRAIL

OREGON TRAIL

Platte River

Ft. Kearney

OREGON TRAIL

OREGON TRAIL

KANSAS

IOWA

Council Bluffs

MORMON TRAIL

Omaha

Missouri River

MISSOURI

St. Joseph

Ft. Leavenworth

Westport Landing
(Kansas City)

Independence

A

GENERAL CIRCULAR

TO ALL

PERSONS OF GOOD CHARACTER,

WHO WISH TO EMIGRATE

TO THE

OREGON TERRITORY,

EMBRACING SOME ACCOUNT OF THE CHARACTER AND
ADVANTAGES OF THE COUNTRY; THE RIGHT
AND THE MEANS AND OPERATIONS BY
WHICH IT IS TO BE SETTLED;—

AND

ALL NECESSARY DIRECTIONS FOR BECOMING

AN EMIGRANT.

Hall J. Kelley, *General Agent.*

BY ORDER OF THE AMERICAN SOCIETY FOR ENCOURAGING

the SETTLEMENT of the OREGON TERRITORY.

INSTITUTED IN BOSTON, A. D. 1829.

CHARLESTOWN:
PRINTED BY WILLIAM W. WHEILDON.
R. P. & C. WILLIAMS—BOSTON.
1831.

"**June 1** [1853] It has been raining all day long, the men and boys are soaking wet . . . and comfortless," wrote Amelia Knight going west on the Oregon Trail in a swaying, ox-drawn "prairie schooner," a canvas-covered wagon " . . . and all this for Oregon," she complained.

Averaging about fifteen miles a day, Amelia, her husband, and seven children had left Iowa for the Oregon Territory two months before. Like most families heading west they had begun their four- to five-month journey by joining a wagon train—a group of prairie schooners—at one of several jumping-off places along the Missouri River. The major jumping-off spots were St. Joseph, Liberty, Westport, and Independence, Missouri. The pioneers aimed to leave in the spring so as to reach Oregon's fertile Willamette Valley before winter.

The Oregon Trail saw its greatest activity during the 1840s and 1850s. Over these twenty years the trail was packed with people and their wagons and animals heading west seeking a better or different life from the one they had had. The farmers among them wanted more fertile "free" land. Many were tradesmen and craftsmen driven west by unemployment in the East. They saw opportunities for wealth in the timber, fur, fish, and ore of the Northwest. Some were explorers who were anxious to discover the character of the vast unknown region. A few were adventurers. Others were individualists yearning for more space. There were missionaries who were determined to bring Christianity to the untamed wilderness. And there were those who headed west for their health, thinking that the weather in Oregon or California was better for them. In 1849, the year following the discovery of gold in California, and for the next several years, the Oregon Trail became choked with dreamers seeking their fortunes in the goldfields.

Emigrant family
DENVER PUBLIC LIBRARY, WESTERN HISTORY DEPT.

Underscoring all this was the restless American nature that had been pushing the frontier westward since colonial days.

The Oregon Trail crossed the Great Plains, breached the Rocky Mountains, and reached the Pacific Northwest. Few could imagine the ordeal of the trail before setting out for the "promised land"—Oregon or California.

But waterless and treeless plains, blistering prairie heat, bone-chilling cold, blizzards, and crushing storms could not discourage most of the 300,000 men, women, and children who made up the great American westward migration. River rapids, cliffs, canyons, and mountains could not stop them either, nor could quicksand, insects, rattlesnakes, stampeding buffaloes, mountain lions, and grizzly bears. Not even marauding Indians, cholera, measles, thirst, starvation, and death held back the tide of emigrants.

The majority survived "seeing the elephant," an expression the emigrants created to describe the very worst conditions possible. Starving to death, drowning in quicksand, or dying of cholera was "seeing the elephant." Some turned back. Others wished they had. About 35,000 people died on the way, one person every 17.5 miles. The dead were buried deep in the ground to keep Indians from taking their clothing and wolves from gnawing at their remains. When a grave was impossible, rocks were used to cover the dead. Every trace of the deceased soon disappeared, including the grave marker. The road was littered with broken wheels, smashed or burned wagons, and dead animals. Still the emigrants rode or walked west on the rutted, grave-studded Oregon Trail.

The earliest of these pioneers were called "emigrants" because they left American soil in the East to go to what was then foreign territories in the West—"Oregon Country" and California. California belonged to Mexico until 1846 when it became

Trailside graves, Nevada

11

American territory, achieving statehood in 1850. Oregon, on the other hand, was a vast wilderness over which raged a boundary dispute between Great Britain and the United States, each claiming the region for itself. Beginning in 1841 so many Americans rolled into Oregon Country in covered wagons that in 1846, Great Britain had no choice but to agree to a permanent border at the 49th parallel. This separated British Canada from American soil. From then on, pioneers bound either for Oregon or California were no longer emigrants going to a foreign land. They were pioneers trekking to American land. They were still called "emigrants," however, even though Oregon achieved territorial status in 1848 and became a state in 1859.

The emigrants learned about the land beyond the Missouri River from the fur trappers, sailors, missionaries, mountain men, and adventurers who had been there before them. They all told wild tales about the wondrous world on the other side of the Rockies. They described land so rich and fertile that anything could grow on it without backbreaking effort. They spun stories about fish and game so plentiful that nobody would ever have to worry about food for their tables again. The emigrants heard about thick lumber and pure ore that would put money in their pockets. They listened to tales of rivers and mountains so beautiful and majestic that no artist or poet could amply describe them. These exciting descriptions held out the promise of easy wealth and a satisfying life in a glorious new country.

French fur trappers called the region "Ouragon" during the 1600s. A French word for "hurricane," *Ouragon* possibly described the violent storms that thundered through the region's mountains. Englishmen in the Canadian Northwest changed Ouragon to Oregon during the 1760s. Oregon encompassed all or parts of British Columbia in Canada and the present-day states of Oregon, Washington, Idaho, Montana, and Wyoming. Mexican land—Utah, Great Basin (Nevada), and California—bordered on Oregon's southern flank.

America claimed Oregon Country in 1792 when an American captain, Robert Gray, sailed his ship *Columbia* up the Oregon River. He renamed it the "Columbia River" in honor of his ship. The river flowed westward into the Pacific Ocean from the Rocky Mountains. Between the Rocky Mountains and the Missouri River sprawled the Great Plains, otherwise known as the "Great American Desert."

This vast plain was the northern piece of the Louisiana Purchase, the deal made in 1803 between American President Thomas Jefferson and the soon-to-be-French Emperor Napoleon Bonaparte. Jefferson and most Americans dreamed of possessing the foreign-held territories on their borders. Na-

Robert Gray

poleon, having given up his dream of an empire on the North American continent, now needed money to finance his conquest of Europe. Thus a $15-million deal was struck. The United States bought over 825,000 square miles of French North America for $18.18 a square mile and pushed the American frontier westward across the Mississippi River to the eastern slopes of the Rocky Mountains. But little was known about the region. Jefferson wasted no time. He appointed his secretary, Captain Meriwether Lewis, and Lieutenant William Clark, Lewis's close friend, to jointly lead an expedition to explore the Louisiana Territory.

In May of the following year, 1804, Lewis and Clark set out for the Northwest. The most important part of the expedition was to map a practical overland route to the Pacific Ocean. The expedition was also to report on the region's natural resources, geography, and people. Hopefully, trade arrangements could be made with the Native Americans who lived there.

Guided by Sacagawea, a Shoshone Indian woman who knew the region, Lewis and Clark took their expedition beyond the western fringe of the Louisiana Purchase territory. They crossed the Continental Divide, the spine of the Rockies that separated eastward-flowing rivers from westward-flowing rivers, and reached the Pacific Ocean at the mouth of the Columbia River. They returned two years later with information and descriptions of a bountiful and beautiful land.

" . . . from the reflection of the sun on the sprey or mist which arrises from these falls there is a beautiful rainbow produced which adds not a little to the beauty of this majectically grand senery . . . this truly magnificent and sublimely grand object . . ." Meriwether Lewis wrote in his journal on June 13, 1805. The next day he observed: ". . . hearing a

THE LOUISIANA TERRITORY 1803

area purchased from France

area returned to England in 1818

area returned to Spain in 1819

Lewis & Clark Expedition, 1804–1806

CANADA

Lake of the Woods

WASHINGTON

Columbia River

OREGON

IDAHO

MONTANA

NORTH DAKOTA

MINNESOTA

Lake Superior

MICHIGAN

Lake Michigan

WISCONSIN

WYOMING

SOUTH DAKOTA

IOWA

NEVADA

Great Salt Lake

COLORADO

NEBRASKA

ILLINOIS

INDIANA

CALIFORNIA

UTAH

KANSAS

St. Louis

MISSOURI

KENTUCKY

ARIZONA

NEW MEXICO

OKLAHOMA

ARKANSAS

TENNESSEE

PACIFIC OCEAN

TEXAS

LOUISIANA

MISSISSIPPI

ALABAMA

MEXICO

GULF OF MEXICO

LEONARD EVERETT FISHER

tremendous roaring above me . . . was again presented by one of the most beautiful objects in nature, a cascade of about fifty feet perpendicular . . . if a skillful painter had been asked to make a beautiful cascade . . . he would . . . have p[r]esented this one; nor could I determine on which of those two great cataracts to bestoe the palm, on this or that which I had discovered yesterday . . . this was pleasingly beautiful . . . the other . . . sublimely grand."

At first, Lewis and Clark's news of the Pacific Northwest fired no one's ambition except that of John Jacob Astor. Astor, a German immigrant, had already made a fortune in the fur trade along the Great Lakes. Now, thanks to Lewis and Clark, he imagined a fur trading empire in the Pacific Northwest.

Astor organized the Pacific Fur Company and sent an expedition by sea, around South America's Cape Horn, to the

Astoria, 1839

mouth of the Columbia River. There, in 1811, his agents established a trading post called "Astoria." The venture nearly failed when the expedition ship blew up after an Indian attack. Fortunately, another Astor expedition stumbled into Astoria after picking its way over the Rocky Mountains, down to the Columbia River. In June of the following year, 1812, a small group of Astoria men, led by Robert Stuart, set out to report to Astor the progress of the venture. After first being helped by friendly Indians, they were later nearly stranded in the Rocky Mountains when hostile Indians stole their horses.

Determined to survive and make their report, Stuart and his men walked on, looking for an easy route through the Rockies. On October 22, 1812, they found a passage through the mountains at the southern end of the Wind River Range in Wyoming. It was so wide and flat that horses and wagons could manage it with ease. That saddle of land across the

Fort George at Astoria, 1841
Drawing by Lt. Charles Wilkes

spine of the Rockies was a bridge between east and west. It was as if sloping ramps had been placed on each side to make a comfortable west-east (or east-west) transit through the mountains. Eventually called "South Pass," it became the gateway through the Rockies for the thousands of eastern pioneers who later went west on the Oregon Trail.

Stuart continued eastward, noting his position every step of the way. He and his party arrived in St. Louis, Missouri, in March 1813. Little did Stuart realize that his west-to-east business trip had marked off the historic Oregon Trail that so many easterners would someday take to Oregon.

In May 1830, three mountain men, Jedediah Smith, David E. Jackson, and William Sublette, left St. Louis, Missouri, with ten wagons full of supplies for trappers on the eastern slopes of the Rockies. They were the first wagon train to travel westward on the Oregon Trail. They reached the mountains and returned to St. Louis about three months later. The three men knew that they had achieved a remarkable first and were convinced that they could have taken the wagons through the Rocky Mountains all the way to Oregon and the Pacific Ocean.

During the Panic of 1837, when the United States and nearly everyone in it seemed penniless, a wealthy Scottish explorer decided to travel the Oregon Trail. He hired an artist, Alfred Jacob Miller, to go with him. Miller's job was to paint the scenes along the way as a record of the trip. Miller returned with paintings and drawings of life in the Far West that gave Americans their first glimpse of what the region, its people, and wildlife looked like. Spectacular outcroppings or gorges like Courthouse Rock, Chimney Rock, and Scottsbluff, Nebraska; Independence Rock and Devil's Gate, Wyoming; came vividly to life. By 1857 other American artists had found their way west, too. Among them was Albert Bierstadt who

Robert Stuart

"Chimney Rock" by A.J. Miller, 1837

WALTERS ART GALLERY, BALTIMORE, MARYLAND

21

"Scottsbluff" by A.J. Miller

WALTERS ART GALLERY, BALTIMORE, MARYLAND

"The Rocky Mountains, Lander's Peak" by Albert Bierstadt, 1863

captured the natural wonders of his journey with huge canvases of the Rocky Mountains under colorful western skies.

Many farmers and shopkeepers lost their farms, shops, and livelihoods in the Panic of 1837. Suddenly, the untamed western wilderness represented an opportunity for a new and successful life. The idea of trekking west into the unknown resembled the Pilgrims' arrival in the Massachusetts wilderness in 1620. "Oregon fever!" hit the country like a plague.

John L. O'Sullivan, a New York newspaperman, wrote in 1845 that it was "our manifest destiny" to own and govern all of North America. These lands belong to America, he reasoned, because Americans had a vision of the lands being one continent, one nation—the American nation. He was referring directly to the Republic of Texas which was about to become a state, as well as Mexican provinces in the Far West and the "Oregon Question" in the Northwest. He was appealing indirectly to the restless energy of the American people who were constantly on the move from east to west, slowly pushing the American frontier toward the Pacific Ocean. The idea of "manifest destiny" caught on. Thousands of farming families from neighboring states who had jammed into Missouri seeking new opportunities and found none took the Oregon Trail to the "promised land" and new lives.

"Oregon or bust!" they all cried.

It mattered little that Oregon lay on the other side of the Rocky Mountains, which many thought impassable. Enough people remembered that South Pass, a way through that lofty wall, had been found in 1812 by Robert Stuart.

"With fond hopes we pictured the beautiful Willamette Valley beyond," recalled one emigrant woman. "The peaks of the mountains . . . caused many an anxious thought . . ."

As early as 1831 a book was published on Oregon giving *All*

Necessary Directions for Becoming an Emigrant. The author, Hall Jackson Kelley, had never been there. Still, he described the wonders of Oregon and its scenic beauty as if he had! He eventually made the trip—by sea! Kelley was a Boston schoolteacher who campaigned endlessly for the United States to take over Oregon. He also dreamed of converting the Indians in Oregon to Christianity. Many Indians, however, had already learned about Christianity from members of the Lewis and Clark expedition. In their minds Christianity gave the white man his guns, wagons, and medicines, which in turn made the white man very powerful.

In 1834, Jason Lee, a young Methodist minister, was determined to convert the Indians, too. He took the trail to Oregon but soon gave up. He preferred to colonize the land with white settlers instead. Two other ministers followed Lee to

Jason Lee
 OREGON HISTORICAL SOCIETY

Oregon. They were Samuel Parker, a Congregationalist, and Marcus Whitman, a Presbyterian. Whitman was also a doctor who spent much of his journey on the Oregon Trail removing arrowheads from the backs of mountain men, treating accident victims, and trying to quell outbreaks of cholera. Whitman returned to the East in 1836 to marry. He came back to Oregon with his bride to preach to and doctor the Cayuse Indians near Fort Walla Walla, Washington. From 1836 to 1847, Marcus Whitman nearly succeeded in bringing Christianity and civilization to the Cayuse.

During those years, the Cayuse had become increasingly disturbed by the thousands of settlers who were colonizing their land. Indian hostility caused a number of Christian missions to return east. In November 1847, an epidemic of measles among the Cayuse wiped out half their tribe. They blamed Whitman and murdered him together with his wife and oth-

Whitman Mission drawn from memory by Nancy A. (Osborn) Jacobs, 1847

ers at the mission. The murders so angered the settlers that they attacked the Cayuse and drove them from the region.

During Marcus Whitman's mission years the United States government sent young Lieutenant John Charles Frémont on expeditions to the West. In 1842, 1843, and again in 1844, Frémont explored much of the Oregon Trail. He sent back detailed reports on its condition, weather, and general environment. He also suggested where the government might build army posts. Frémont's explorations and enthusiasm caused additional waves of excitement among thousands of restless Americans.

"Oregon societies" sprang up everywhere. Contracts were signed between the organizers and those who wanted to go to Oregon. Wagon trains were organized. Leaders or "captains" were elected by the emigrants themselves. Later the "wagon master" took charge of the wagon train. His word was the law.

Lieutenant John Charles Frémont
NATIONAL ARCHIVES

Rules of conduct were spelled out. Lectures were given on how to create a campsite of wagons and how to draw the wagons in a circle or square for protection against attack. Experienced "pilots" or scouts who knew the Oregon Trail were hired by the multitude gathering along the Missouri River to guide the wagon trains safely to Oregon.

"It is estimated that the company . . . will consist of . . . one thousand persons, one hundred wagons, and about two thousand cattle . . ." reported the *St. Joseph* [Missouri] *Gazette* on May 2, 1845, " . . . and the whole wealth of the company is near one hundred thirty thousand dollars . . ."

Hundreds of pounds of food were stored in the supply wagons—flour, grain, bacon, salt, coffee, sugar, dried fruits, pickles, and so on. There had to be enough horses, rifles, pistols, and ammunition "for every male over 18 years of age." Spare parts, tools, medicines and tonics, cooking ware, plates and eating utensils were packed in a family's wagon.

"There is space in the middle of the wagon, the bottom is carpeted, two chairs and a mirror make it appear like a home," wrote one immigrant in 1845.

As noted, one wagon train could consist of a thousand men, women, and children, as many as three thousand to four thousand head of cattle, pet dogs and cats, and more than a hundred wagons. At times, these trains formed a line five miles long. They were the largest outdoor camping caravans ever seen in America!

While the courage of the emigrants was the heartbeat of the wagon trains, the white-canvased, bright blue, red-wheeled prairie schooners were their symbol. They were not the tough, canvas-covered Conestoga wagons that nudged the eastern frontier westward before 1850. These earlier wagons were first built in Conestoga, Pennsylvania, around 1725. Dubbed

The inside of a wagon

Henry Smith Family

DENVER PUBLIC LIBRARY, WESTERN HISTORY DEPT.

"camels of the prairies," they were drawn by teams of four to six horses or mules. They were too clumsy to take across the sharp and steep mountainous areas. Also, they were too heavy to be lowered by ropes from high cliffs to lower ground, a maneuver that many found necessary in the mountains.

Experience quickly taught the emigrants that a smaller, lighter wagon would be better. These newer wagons, some fourteen or fifteen feet long, were straighter, narrower, and just as durable as the Conestogas. One emigrant described his wagon as "narrow . . . the hoops over which the cover is laid, is bent so as to make the top almost flat. The cover is cotton drilling, two thicknesses, the outside oiled. The outside cloth comes down below the bottom on the end boards, so as to admit no rain . . ."

They were made sturdy by the same hardwoods used in the Conestogas. They boasted the same huge, reliable iron-tired

OREGON HISTORICAL SOCIETY

wheels, but were usually drawn by teams of four oxen. The oxen were not only better suited for pulling heavily loaded wagons, they were more manageable than mules or horses. Mules and horses were used chiefly as pack and riding animals. If the oxen gave out, then the mules were hitched to the wagons.

Usually, the day began at sunup. The cows were milked. Breakfast was cooked and eaten. Dishes were washed and stored. The oxen were yoked to the wagon and the wagon train was ready to move by eight o'clock. Noon was lunchtime and the wagon train came to a halt. After a couple of hours of eating and resting, the wagon train continued its journey until the early evening—about five o'clock—when a suitable campsite was found. Eight wagons called a "mess" were arranged in a circle. There could be a dozen such circular encampments in one wagon train. The oxen were unhitched. Supper was cooked and eaten. Afterward, people either read their Bibles, prayed, listened to a sermon, if a minister happened to be along, played cards, or sang songs around a campfire. Guards were posted throughout the night. By dawn of the next day they were ready to move on.

Water, fodder, cattle feed, and campfire fuels—wood or buffalo dung called "chips"—were picked up along the way. Too often good drinking water could not be found. Driven by heat and unbearable thirst to drinking brackish, often poisonous water, many became sick and died. "Passed five graves this morning," wrote a pioneer woman in 1852, ". . . passed two graves today . . . one young lady died last night . . . the other could live but a few hours longer . . . both sisters . . . their father had buried his wife, one brother, one sister, two sons in law . . ."

Those who got an early spring start in April had little trouble feeding their animals on the new grasses along the way. But those who left later in May found no grass left for their animals. If they did not wander far off the trail to graze their cattle, the cattle died. As the emigrants wandered from side to side looking for grazing opportunities for the thousands of head of cattle that they were moving westward, the course of the Oregon Trail changed from time to time. A late spring or early summer start also put a slow-moving wagon train at the mercy of the snows that came early to the Rocky Mountains.

Such a nightmare touched the eighty-seven men, women, and children who made up the Donner-Reed wagon train. This California-bound group of emigrants had left Independence, Missouri, in May 1846. They bumped along the Oregon Trail as far as Fort Bridger, Wyoming, a trading post established in 1842 by Jim Bridger, a trapper. There they turned south, taking a shortcut that more experienced mountain men advised against. By August they were south of the Great Salt Lake and moving toward the Sierra Nevada Mountains.

Once in the mountains, the going became slower, tougher, and colder. By the time they hit the eastern slopes of the Sierras in late October, they were bucking snowstorms and drifts at least five feet high. Wagons in the rear could not keep up and began to drop back. The wagons began to separate from one another. The deep snow made further progress impossible. The emigrants tried to make camp and protect themselves against the howling winds and drifts. They built makeshift shelters out of fallen timber, and even found a vacant cabin. The snow continued to fall. By November they were trapped, covered by some fifteen feet of snow with drifts as high as forty feet.

One by one their animals wandered off or froze to death.

Jim Bridger, photo by C.W. Carter

All during December and January the emigrants fought frost-bite, starvation, and the hopelessness of their situation. They began to die, too. Fifteen of them made an attempt to seek help. Eight never made it. Little by little the starving emigrants began to eat the flesh of their own dead. By the time they were rescued in late February, forty-five of the original eighty-seven emigrants were still alive.

One of the largest groups to emigrate in the 1840s were the Mormons. A religious group fleeing persecution, they set out for the West in 1846 from Nauvoo, Illinois, a town they had established in 1839. Mobs who resented their beliefs and had murdered their leader, Joseph Smith, hounded them out of Illinois. In April 1847, seventy-three Mormon wagons guided by Brigham Young, their new leader, crossed the Missouri River near Council Bluffs, Iowa. They crawled along the north side of the Platte River within sight of emigrant wagons on the south side. Their road to the West came to be known as the "Mormon Trail." On the way they erected signposts to guide others of their faith to their destination, the Utah Territory.

Altogether, the Oregon Trail spanned about two thousand miles. Three or four weeks after the emigrants left their jumping-off point on the Missouri River, they reached Fort Kearney on the south bank of the Platte River. From Fort Kearney, the trail worked its way upland toward the Rocky Mountains. Three or four weeks later, after traveling another three hundred to four hundred miles northwest along the south bank of the Platte River, the emigrants reached Fort Laramie.

Nearing Fort Laramie in what is now the state of Wyoming, Amelia Knight wrote: **"June 11** . . . crossed . . . the most desolate piece of ground that was ever made . . . not a drop of water, nor a spear of grass . . . nothing but barren hills, bare

Brigham Young

Mormon wagon train

and broken rock, sand and dust."

Beyond Fort Laramie, following the North Platte and Sweetwater rivers upland, the Oregon Trail reached the Continental Divide. There, the wagon trains eased through the Continental Divide at South Pass and more often than not began their steep, downhill trip to Fort Bridger. It was here that the Mormons and the Oregon emigrants went separate ways.

"We took the left-hand road that leads to California," wrote William Clayton, the Mormon record keeper.

Some of the Oregon wagons took Sublette's Cutoff halfway between the western slope of South Pass and Fort Bridger. Sublette's Cutoff saved time and distance for a wagon train bound for the Northwest.

Fort Laramie, Nebraska, 1858 (earliest known photograph) LIBRARY OF CONGRESS

While the Mormons and, later, the gold seekers turned south to Utah and California, the emigrants continued northwest. They passed Soda Springs, Idaho with its bubbling mineral waters. Farther on was Fort Hall, Idaho, a trading post established in 1834 by Nathaniel Wyeth, a New England fur merchant. If the emigrants had a change of heart and decided to go to California instead, they took a trail either from Soda Springs or Fort Hall, southwest across the Sierra Nevada Mountains to California.

Oregon-bound emigrants continued northwest from Fort Hall. They followed the south side of the Snake River for about 250 miles before crossing over to the north side. The two-hundred-yard crossing was made difficult by treacherous currents and varying depths of fast-moving water. Groups of wagons had to be chained together, one behind the other, while extra teams of oxen alternately swam and walked as they pulled the heavily loaded wagons through the water. The wagons were guided across the river by horsemen who kept

Fort Hall, Idaho, artist unknown, 1849
OREGON HISTORICAL SOCIETY

Emigrant wagon train

the oxen heading in the right direction. The wagons themselves were made as watertight as possible by having their cracks stuffed with clothing or cloth sheets soaked in tar or pitch. Most of the supplies and family possessions inside the wagon were either piled high off the wagon floor to keep them dry or unloaded altogether and put on a raft. At times the wagon wheels were well above the water. And just as suddenly they would disappear into deep water, flooding the wagon's interior. One emigrant wrote that they had to "...ferry the wagons over. Had to take them apart and float the box (i.e. the wagon without its wheels)... got some groceries wet, some coffee, sugar dissolved..."

One hundred miles later the emigrants were in Fort Boise, Idaho. Ahead were the Blue Mountains, the Whitman Mission, Fort Walla Walla, the Columbia River, and The Dalles— a stretch of river rapids. Finally, they reached the end of the

Main Street, Boise, Idaho, 1866
IDAHO HISTORICAL SOCIETY

Sheridan Point Cascades, Columbia River Gorge, 1860

The Dalles, Oregon, 1867
OREGON HISTORICAL SOCIETY

The Dalles, Oregon, 1864

Oregon Trail at Fort Vancouver. Nearby was the beautiful Willamette Valley, the embodiment of the dream that had kept them going for so many months.

As if the huge job of moving a wagon train across rivers and over mountains to Oregon was not enough, the trail west and through the Rockies was lined with Indians whose response to the migration was sometimes hostile.

"The Arapahoe Indians . . . profess to be friendly to the whites," wrote Edward Everett Hale in 1854, "but the safer policy is to give them a wide berth . . . The Cheyenne are in alliance with the Arapahoes, professing friendship, but very treacherous." Hale was a Boston clergyman and editor who would win everlasting fame with his book *The Man Without a Country.*

Five years later, in 1859, an American army captain, Randolph B. Marcy, wrote, "Their [i.e., Indians] tactics are such as to render the old system of warfare useless . . . he who can count the greatest number of scalps is the most highly favored . . . the young warrior often is anxious to attack the white settlers . . . these young braves should, therefore be closely watched . . . A small number of white men, in traveling upon the Plains, should not allow a party of strange Indians to approach them."

Except for large clusters of Indian nations and grazing buffalo herds, the entire region west of the Missouri was so vast that it seemed vacant. A handful of United States Army troops patrolled the frontier. These cavalry regiments hardly made a dent in the utter loneliness of the region. There were never enough troopers to defend the wagon trains against Indian attacks.

". . . there was suddenly heard a shot and a blood curdling yell . . . the Indians kept circling . . . bullets came whizzing

Looking Glass from the Nez Percé tribe

through the camp. None can know the horror of it . . . ," wrote a young bride on her wedding trip west in a covered wagon. There were no soldiers within earshot of that attack.

". . . Indians . . . stopped the teams, but appeared friendly, shaking hands and asking for whiskey . . . while . . . talking of trading they opened fire on us. My uncle was killed outright . . . my father's teamster was shot, my father was shot . . . The Indians also killed all the men in the forward party . . . the women and children . . . burned by the savages."

"Our little army," wrote Captain Marcy, "scattered as it has been . . . in small garrisons of one or two companies each, has seldom been in a position to act . . ."

The forts that dotted the region were primarily trading posts. In 1846 there were no United States troops closer than seven hundred miles to the east of Fort Laramie. Fort Laramie, first called Fort William, had been established by the

Fort Leavenworth, Kansas, from an 1849 drawing

American Fur Company in 1834. The forts did not become military posts until later when a growing white population that had settled on land with United States "territorial" status needed to be protected from warring Indians. Fort Laramie, for example, became a United States military post in 1849 and remained one until 1890.

The forts were oases in the middle of nowhere. They depended on the scheduled arrival of supply wagons to maintain their connection with civilization and to stay stocked with food and arms. As long as the forts traded food, clothing, and whiskey to the surrounding Indians there was usually peace.

Native Americans on both sides of the Rockies—the Pawnee, Arapaho, Kiowa, Cheyenne, Sioux, Kansas, Crow, and Blackfoot on one side; the Bannock, Gosiute, Paiute, Shoshone, Nez Percé, Cayuse, and Yakima on the other side—had good reason to be wary of the wagons pressing westward along the Oregon Trail, swelling the population of the Northwest. Hungry for food, the pioneers mercilessly slaughtered the buffalo, depriving Native Americans of food and clothing.

The Crow and Blackfoot, especially, were forever suspicious of the white man's invasion of their ancestral lands. From time to time they sent a cruel warning to trespassers by attacking lonely trappers and hunters, scalping them or torturing them to death.

Even those Native Americans who were friendly and helpful kept the emigrants on edge whenever they came around to trade. On more than one occasion emigrants would trade a gun for a horse only to find that the Indian trader had returned to retrieve his horse in the middle of the night. The Pawnees made a habit of quietly sneaking into camp in the dark of the night to steal cows, horses, guns, blankets, and provisions of all kinds. They were so skillful at their pilfering that they could take a blanket off a sleeping person without alerting the guard or arousing the sleeper!

Amelia Knight, continuing in her diary, wrote: "**July 18th** . . . Crossed one small creek and have camped on one called Rock Creek. It is here the Indians are so troublesome . . . I was very much frightened . . . I lay awake all night. I expected every minute we would be killed . . . There are people killed at this place every year."

Most Native Americans believed that since the land belonged to no one it was not the white man's to take—or to give, for that matter. Americans moving west believed the land was free, theirs for the taking because Native Americans never worked the land nor produced anything from it. Frustrated and angry, tribe after tribe warred against wagon trains, railroads, settlements, and the army, spreading death and destruction whenever and wherever they could. Women and children were sometimes dragged off by marauding Indians.

Emigrant Camp (engraving)
OREGON HISTORICAL SOCIETY

A few of the victims turned up later—years later—having escaped their captors. Others were never seen or heard from again.

Many Native Americans were surprisingly friendly, however. Some were eager to help. One emigrant recalled years later that the "Indians were peaceable all along the route." Another insisted that they "never molested us at any time." In a number of instances Indians maintained a going business of rafting the emigrants and their wagons across rivers. The rate was about three dollars a wagon.

As the emigrants neared trading posts on the Oregon Trail like Fort Laramie, they looked for protection and safety. But once inside they were astonished to see Indians wandering in and out of the stockade.

"Tall Indians . . . were striding across the area or reclining at full length on the low roofs of the building which enclosed it (i.e. Fort Laramie). Numerous squaws sat grouped in front of the rooms they occupied; their . . . offspring . . . rambled in every direction through the fort; and the trappers, traders . . . of the establishment were busy at their labor or their amusements," wrote Francis Parkman in 1847 in his book, *The Oregon Trail*. Parkman was describing Fort Laramie as it had been the previous year.

A recent graduate of Harvard College in Cambridge, Massachusetts, Parkman decided to learn all he could about Western Indians, "Having from childhood felt a curiosity on the subject . . ." The twenty-three-year-old Parkman journeyed across the Oregon Trail in 1846 with a friend, Quincy A. Shaw. Upon their return, Parkman's health was so bad that he had to dictate the entire book to Shaw.

"The little fort [i.e., Laramie] is built of bricks dried in the sun," Parkman continued, ". . . an oblong form, with . . . clay

Fort Laramie Interior by A.J. Miller, 1837

. . . blockhouses at two of the corners. The walls are about 15 feet high . . . surmounted by a slender palisade . . . the apartments within . . . are built close against the walls . . . The main entrance has two gates with an arched passage intervening. A little square window, high above the ground, opens into this passage; so that when the inner gate is closed and barred, a person without may still hold communication with those within."

The forts did provide some comfort for the weary pioneers. They could rest from their difficult trip and prepare for the ordeals ahead. They could take on fresh provisions, care for the sick and injured, and tend to their animals. They could clean and repair everything, from clothing and rifles to soleless boots and broken wagon wheels.

During the Civil War years, 1861–1865, the trail was nearly empty of the long and crowded wagon trains. Most of the men were called to serve either in the Union or Confederate armies. Too few men were free to make the trek to Oregon or California. When the war ended, the wagon trains began to move out again but not in as great numbers as before. Now railroads and stage coaches could speedily carry large numbers of people from east to west and back again. By the turn of the century, 1900, the great wagon trains on the Oregon Trail were no longer to be seen.

But as the Civil War overtook the eastern part of America, greatly reducing the number of covered wagons on the Oregon Trail, a new sight and sound emerged on the trail. From April 3, 1860 to October 24, 1861, the Oregon Trail between St. Joseph, Missouri, and Fort Bridger felt the pounding hooves of the Pony Express. Few single events at the time so captured the imagination of the country as the daredevil riders who moved the mail across the western wilderness.

The mail reached St. Joseph from the East by rail. From that point it was taken by about 25 young men. Riding some 135 horses in relays, at breakneck speeds, they traveled nonstop across the Oregon Trail to Fort Bridger; then they left the trail and rode through the mountains to Sacramento, California—a distance of 2,000 miles. The same number of riders and horses went the other way.

The first trip took ten days, a far cry from the four to five months or more of the wagon train. The Pony Express was replaced by the coast-to-coast telegraph a year and a half later. By that time the daring riders who braved every danger known along the route from blizzards to Indians had cut the time down to eight days.

To some, the Oregon Trail was an unforgettable adventure despite the hardships. To others, it was a nightmare from beginning to end. No description could aptly describe either the adventure or the ordeal of the Oregon Trail. The iron will and strength of character shown by Americans who went west in covered wagons is almost beyond belief. They were determined to get to the "promised land."

"Our journey across the Plains was a long and hard one," wrote one emigrant to a relative back east. "We lost everything but our lives."

And many lost everything, including their lives.

Mother and child just after arrival in northeast Washington

Wagon train in the Rocky Mountains

Index

(Italicized numbers indicate pages with photos.)

Chimney Rock
OREGON HISTORICAL SOCIETY

ACKNOWLEDGMENTS

Leonard Everett Fisher would like to thank Doris Kimmel for her invaluable help in researching photos for this book; also, Susan Seyl, Photographs Librarian at the Oregon Historical Society; Jerry Kearns of the Photo Duplication Service of the Library of Congress; Susan Cook of Smithsonian Institution Press; and the Western History Department of the Denver Public Library for their guidance and quick responses to requests for photos and information; and Shannon Maughan for her special assistance in coordinating the project.

Mr. Fisher would also like to thank the following organizations for granting permission to use their photographs: The Butler Institute of American Art, jacket front; The Church of Jesus Christ of Latter-Day Saints, page 40; Denver Public Library, Western History Department, pages 8, 32, 62; Frederic Remington Art Museum, page 2; Idaho Historical Society, page 45; Kansas Historical Society, page 37; Library of Congress, pages 11, 39, 42; The Metropolitan Museum of Art, page 24; Missouri Historical Society, page 19; National Archives, pages 29, 31, 44, 53; Oregon Historical Society, pages 6, 13, 16, 17, 27, 28, 34, 43, 46, 48, 50, 56, 61, 64; State Historical Society of Wisconsin, page 54; Utah State Historical Society, page 1; The Walters Art Gallery, pages 20, 22, 58.

Mr. Fisher prepared the maps on pages 4-5, and 15.

Library of Congress Cataloging-in-Publication Data
Fisher, Leonard Everett.
The Oregon Trail / by Leonard Everett Fisher. — 1st ed.
p.   cm.
Summary: Charts the journey of those who followed the Oregon Trail
in the first half of the nineteenth century, describes the obstacles
and dangers they encountered, and discusses the Trail's eventual
decline with the introduction of the cross-country railroad.
ISBN 0-8234-0833-7
1. Oregon Trail—Juvenile literature.
2. Overland journeys to the Pacific—Juvenile literature.
3. West (U.S.)—Description and travel—1848–1860—Juvenile literature.
4. West (U.S.)—Description and travel—1860–1880—Juvenile literature.
[1. Oregon Trail. 2. Overland journeys to the Pacific.
3. West (U.S.)—History. 4. Frontier and pioneer life.] I. Title.
F597.F57 1990
979.5'03—dc20   90-55103   CIP   AC